30 Days of Pleasure

National Bestselling Author
SIERRA KAY

The Vega Group
Chicago, Illinois

30 Days of Pleasure
Copyright © 2021 Sierra Kay

This is a work of fiction. Names, characters, places, and incidents are products of the author's imagination or are used fictitiously and are not to be construed as real. Any resemblance to actual events, locales, organizations, or persons, living, dead, or somewhere in between is entirely coincidental.

Ebook ISBN: 9781952871191
Published by Macro Publishing Group

Trade Paperback ISBN: 978-0-9997759-7-4
Published by The Vega Group

All rights reserved. No part of this book may be used or reproduced in any manner whatsoever or by any means including electronic, mechanical or photocopying, or stored in a retrieval system without written permission of the author, except in the case of brief quotations embodied in critical articles and reviews. For permission, contact Stephanie M. Freeman at gmail.com or at www.naleighnakai.com

Cover Designed by: J.L Woodson: www.woodsoncreativestudio.com
Interior Designed by: Lissa Woodson: www.naleighnakai.com
Editor: Naleighna Kai
Betas: Debra Mitchell and Kelsie Maxwell

30 Days of Pleasure

National Bestselling Author
SIERRA KAY

♦ DEDICATION ♦

This book is dedicated to my fellow creatives, including my Aunt Shirley, who knows no limits, sees no boxes, and continues to push boundaries with boundless energy. Stay amazing.

Chapter 1

His fingers teased her with the briefest flutter causing her senses to reach out in search of the next touch that drew a design of desire across her skin.

The hand grasped her leg as if her right thigh was the only thing standing between him and salvation. Although her body dripped with desire accentuated by the muscles of his chest branding into her back, it wasn't enough. She needed so much more.

Alicia's mind released all decision-making to the needs of her body. It knew how to talk when language was all but forgotten. Her thigh lifted slightly, giving him both an invitation and access to the essence of her being. The slightest nibble on her ear sent a shockwave searing through her nerves. Fire from their coupling consumed all the oxygen in the room, causing her to pant as she tried for sounds that could possibly lead to words.

Until the deep timbre of his voice echoed in her ear, "Hey, Suga."

Alicia Mitchell's body jackknifed from a deep sensual sleep to wide awake. She brushed the hair back from her face as she scanned every inch of the room. Breathing proved harder in her wakened state because the voice she heard in the depth of slumber didn't belong to Dallas Avery; the man currently keeping her body humming and making good sense a distant memory.

The body was definitely his. The touch and her reaction—his. But the voice? No. That voice belonged to Taric Hasan. Taric existed in her life prior to Dallas. It only took a couple of encounters before she realized Taric's charm could only lead a woman one place—the grave. That's someplace Alicia chose to avoid until God deemed her journey over. Clearly, the fact that she caught Taric releasing one poor soul from their mortal coil meant God had other plans for her. What she didn't escape were the nightmares that reminded her of the narrow blade separating life and death.

Heart pounding with a slight sheen of sweat covering her body, she scanned every inch of the room again. She tried to convince her mind that she was safe. Fear held on tighter than skinny jeans after a holiday meal.

Her visual survey indicated no immediate threat. She strained to hear any man-made sound, but only heard the hum of the air conditioner and the faint ding of the elevator in the hall. With hand over heart, she implored it to calm down.

Logically, her fear didn't make sense. She'd left her hometown of Chicago and by association, Taric, to travel.

Only a dream. Only a nightmare. Just like her brief relationship with Taric. His southern drawl initially brought to mind sweet tea and peach cobbler. That ended when she walked into his apartment, lined with plastic without one paint can in sight. Just Taric, a knife, and a female who'd been dead by the time Alicia sprinted out the same way she came in, to call the police.

Taric had never been found. Of course, she knew so little about him. Taric wasn't his real name. His cell phone. Burner. His background was apparently a thing of fairy tales. The dark fairy tales with trolls under bridges and witches behind every tree.

These nightmares were the reason why she stayed in her hotel room instead of Dallas' suite. When she woke, she needed to see and hear her environment. Strange how some spaces were now too big for her alone.

Alicia understood the delicate balance of life. Now, she sagged against the pillows and reminisced about its strange turns. She'd met Taric online, where everyone flocked to find their next forever one. The commercials alone made people believe a genie lived within the computer, granting match wishes.

She'd spent hours responding, blocking, and wondering if she wouldn't have better results with her thumb and a dirt road, until she uncovered the trainer—turned real estate entrepreneur. She hadn't been on a dating site since.

Then on a quick decision to support a friend's charity auction, she'd purchased a dinner with Dallas Avery, a professional basketball player. She thought she'd bid on him, help the cause, get an autograph, and head out for her flight. What started as a cool story she could tell her niece, "One day I went to a charity auction and met NBA star Dallas Avery," turned into a steamy tale that she'd have to tell her best friend over a glass of wine. "One day I went to a charity auction, met Dallas Avery; and gurl, that man …"

Against her better judgment … well, technically she couldn't claim their interlude was against her better judgment because the man overwhelmed every ounce of sense until she melted in his arms. The easiest way to describe the level of physical perfection would be to say if Michelangelo had seen Dallas Avery, he would have thrown the sculpture of David in the trash.

Even though her daily intention continued to be the "flight to anywhere she wanted to go," Dallas was intent on working his way up her priority list by creating memories that would stop her in the middle of her tracks while crossing a busy urban street in broad daylight, plant a smile on her lips, and dampen the delta between her thighs to the point of flooding.

In Dallas' arms, she slept soundly without residual flashes of Taric. Yet, nights like tonight when Dallas was away at a game, the past flooded her brain until all she could do was turn on the television and watch whatever drivel occupied her mind in the middle of the night.

She didn't know much about Dallas, really. He seemed cool. He had a personality which drew her in. That didn't mean he wasn't a psychopath. He may simply hide it better. Their age difference made her a bit suspicious. Though she never felt it was an issue for him.

Alicia jumped at the sudden ringing of her cell phone. At 3 a.m., no one should be calling her. She realized the unknown number could belong to her fabulous daydream. But with her mind still reeling from that voice it conjured, she feared it could also be her chilling nightmare that never quite went away.

Chapter 2

Dallas punched his pillow again as if the fluffy mound held the responsibility for the fact that his mind wouldn't rest so he could sleep. The further he appeared to be from sleep the more frustrated he became, leading him even further from sleep.

He gave up and slid out from underneath the covers. If sleep wouldn't grant his mind reprieve, he'd at least get some work done. His naked body immediately felt the drop in temperature from the warmth of the down comforter to being assaulted by the chill of the air conditioner.

If Alicia had been in the bed with him, he'd never leave it. He couldn't restrain the smile that appeared just at the thought of her. As an NBA player, he had his share of women throwing themselves at him. A few he caught. More he tossed back.

They'd met at a charity auction that he'd only attended at the behest of his mother.

"Isn't it a bit wrong for a mother to try selling her son?" He tried reasoning while his brain sifted through several excuses until it found one that might work. "Don't people go to jail for that?"

She countered, "It's not like that, Dallas, and you know it. All you have to do is take the winning bidder to dinner. That's it. I expect everyone to keep their clothes on and both feet on the floor."

"You said the same thing prom night." Dallas gave a hearty chuckle. "You want details of what happened then?"

"Absolutely not." She choked. "I'm going to continue to believe you went to a 24-hour ice cream shop before you escorted her home."

Confused, Dallas went through his memory banks trying to find the origin of that lie. "I never said I went—"

"Listen," his mother snapped. "It's my story, and I'm sticking to it."

Dallas chuckled. He would allow her to keep her fantasy. Just as he kept the memory of Cassandra Donald locked away in the section of his memory reserved for life experiences that made him say, *Thank you, God.* "So no to reenacting prom night. Got it."

"Dallas, please! Be serious. Your name alone would draw a crowd. That could potentially raise all the bids and bring more interest and press, which would lead to people helping."

Groaning, Dallas tried again. "Mom, can't I just donate? It'll be a good one."

And that's when she unleashed it. The mom guilt. Amazing in its design. Just the question erased everything else in his head making it impossible to formulate a comeback if one lived in the recesses of his brain awaiting just this moment.

"What do I ever ask you for?"

Why did he even bother? "Fine," Dallas acquiesced with a weary sigh. "I'll do it."

"Great," she whooped. "I'll call and set everything up. Just show up with your tux and a smile."

They both knew when she called that he'd fold. He always folded. At least he didn't have to listen to the number of hours she'd been in labor. Plus, with her recent cancer diagnosis, if this is what she wanted of him, of course, he'd do it. He could name worse things to do with his time.

"Yes, ma'am. But," he added. "If your future daughter-in-law ends up being a 75-year-old widow with a bank account full of cash and a desire for a youngster to keep her company then you have no one to blame but yourself."

Laughing, his mother agreed, "Noted."

Alicia's body called out to him the minute he entered the ballroom where the auction was held. The shimmering green fabric rode her curves like a race car driver on the last lap of the Indy 500. The sway of her hips put him under her spell like a pocket watch in the hands of a hypnotist.

The gods were smiling on him when the winning bid turned out to be, Alicia Mitchell, the same woman who had caught his eye the moment he walked into the room. As he made his way toward her that night, every part of his body screamed to be first. His lips wanted to taste her. Hands wanted to hold her. Eyes, well, they wanted access to all that dress promised, but didn't tell.

Giving her the same smile that catapulted women all over the world into his arms, he expected it to be an easy transition from a vertical introduction to a horizontal interlude. And what were her first words? "All I want is a personalized autograph. Dinner isn't necessary."

He felt his own face fall, bounce twice on the ground, and make a rebound back into position before he captured his smile again. "Don't you want to have dinner with the actual man, rather than curl up with a picture?"

Her reply? "No thanks."

Maybe in his rush to get to the auction, he'd forgotten to put on deodorant or had something stuck in his teeth. He felt the energy of women all over the room wanting him. Eyes peeling back his layers just as his eyes peeled back Alicia's. And yet, the one that he desired only wanted an autograph and to catch a red-eye flight out of town.

Dallas worked down her resistance. Although not 75, he did end up with a hot, young widow that night. And looking at the clock, knowing she remained nestled in her room at the Ritz Carlton waiting for him to make it back in town made him almost giddy. Not giddy enough that he couldn't feel that his body temp was steadily falling while he took this trip down memory lane.

Shivering, he went to the closet and pulled out the plush white terry cloth robe generously provided by the hotel. Tying the belt loosely around his hips, he tried to keep his mind off of room service. During the season, he stuck to a diet that kept his body in peak physical condition. He'd read stories of the greatest players in history and how they ate and exercised to extend their time in the league. He gave his best effort, but clearly, those players have never eaten his mother's peach cobbler. That alone was worth extra gym time. And don't get him started on her banana pudding. It would make a man slap his momma. Not him, though. Although he towered over her, he had it on good authority that his mother wouldn't hesitate to lay him out and dig his grave herself. And at the time, he believed her. Her cooking was good, though.

Dallas' stomach growled. Instead of giving in to room service, he made himself a cup of peppermint tea and dialed Alicia's room. Her voice might be the balm he needed to get a few hours of sleep before their plane left for Indiana to play the Pacers.

"Hello?" Her tentative voice made him realize he'd blocked his number when he dialed. Old habit.

"Hey, love. It's Dallas."

Relief echoed when she said, "Oh, thank goodness." Curiosity laced the following words. "Aren't you supposed to be asleep?"

"Yep. I know that. *You* know that. But my brain is too busy solving the world's problems to be troubled with something as mundane as sleep."

"Maybe you should take a shot of something," Alicia suggested.

"I am," he responded, grinning. "You."

He felt her smile through the phone, and the lightness in her voice confirmed it. "No, I meant alcohol."

Dallas gave a low, throaty chuckle. "I like my idea better. You should be here with me. In my bed." His voice deepened in memory. "I love the way you put me to sleep."

"Mmm," Alicia moaned over the phone. "You don't play fair."

"How so?" Dallas asked although he knew exactly what she meant. He'd asked her to join him on this road trip, but she declined, promising to be there when he came back. He felt her resistance. Yet, also felt her desire. That's the part he fed into until she couldn't take anymore. Then he fed her again.

He couldn't blame her, though. Even he admitted that most of his exes ended up on the front cover of one publication or another. It would be hard to keep her a secret if she showed up at every game in every city. But, oh what fun it would be.

She responded, "When you use that voice."

"This is the voice God gave me," he replied, trying—and failing—for his most innocent tone.

"It's like I know you're talking to me, but there's a hidden message that you add that the um, well, makes the crown between my thighs weep for you."

"So you want me? That's what you're saying." Before she responded, his heart rate must have slowed, as all his blood redirected until his robe tented, his body begging for release. However, it desired to be sheathed in Alicia's warmth. No substitution would do.

"I'm saying..." She paused and sighed as if he'd dragged the next words out of her by the threat of violence. But it could only be her desire weaving the tapestry of her words. "I'm saying that I'd love for you to tap gently on my door before you slowly come inside. I'm saying that once you walk through the door, I'd love to feel your weight on top of me while each stroke takes my breath away. I'd love to reach the point where every thought is of the completion that only you drive me to. And when it's over, I'd love to lay in your arms so sated that my muscles refuse to budge until I feel you rise again for a second round."

Dallas almost dropped the phone. Private plane. There had to be a private plane back to Dallas tonight. He'd build one if he necessary.

"But," she added with a devilish tone. "We're just going to have to wait until tomorrow night."

Immediately, he deflated. *Everything deflated.* "Baby, I can make it happen. Maybe I'll tell Coach—"

"Dallas?"

Groaning, he responded, "Yes?"

"I'll be here when you get back. I promise. Good night."

The line disconnected.

Dallas stared at his cell phone as though it was one of those sci-fi portals that would land him next to Alicia. No such luck. Looking down and finding himself erect again he wondered how much would he get fined if he left? He closed his eyes and let her words wash over him from his memory. Damn, that woman knew how to leave an impression. And he was going to have to pay for this robe because it would surely be destroyed after being covered with evidence of his desire for Alicia.

Just one more day, baby.

Chapter 3

Alicia's body felt like jelly after a morning spent at the Ritz Carlton spa. Her legs that so ably walked into the spa wanted to be wheeled back to the bedroom so she could maintain the delicate balance on the cusp of consciousness.

Dallas had given her the key to his suite prior to leaving, as she'd given him a key to hers, but to sleep in that huge room didn't sit well with her. The layout included a bedroom, living room, dining room, office, plus an on-floor concierge dedicated to making her stay a pleasant one.

Although Taric, or whatever his name was, had disappeared like a puff of smoke in a sandstorm, if caught, he'd be tried for that poor woman's murder. The police would drag her back to Chicago to testify.

Her sanity remained in limbo. Could be that she'd never see him again. Could be he lurked around the next corner. The push and pull of her thoughts kept her up at night and coiled her muscles during the day.

So when she laid on the massage table, stress coiled her tendons. Even the masseuse had to press pause on her thoughts.

"Ma'am?" the young, muscular titan inquired. "You're tightening up. Relax."

"Oh, sorry."

Whatever the masseur's name was, would be just the kind of guy that she'd at least flirt with a little, especially since her conversation with Dallas left her almost desperate for release. Almost. However, even now, at the height of horniness, she didn't want to waste an orgasm. Waste it? Like an orgasm was ever wasted. Somehow her mind and body preferred Dallas along for the ride. Unfortunately, he didn't return until the evening. Damn it.

Taking deep breaths, she tried to think of happy, nonsexual, non-psycho thoughts. Sunrises. Rainbows. Laughter. Morning cups of coffee. That time she woke to pour herself a cup of coffee, wearing Dallas' shirt. And by the time she placed the coffee pot back into the maker, he'd lifted the shirt and eased his way inside her, expanding her walls so fully that all she could do was moan.

Thank goodness, she always kept her underwear on during a massage because if not, whatshisname, the masseur, would have to concentrate on her back and shoulders. Or turn the nice safe Swedish massage into a happy ending.

"Much better, ma'am." He kneaded deeper.

Sure. She imitated a glop of chocolate pudding, while her mind continued to ricochet between life and death.

Back in her room, the red light on her phone was on. Calling down to the front desk, they informed her that she had two packages. Dallas. She barely contained her excitement as they were dropped off to her.

Opening the large one revealed a gorgeous black Tom Ford sequined dress with red-bottom high heel shoes. The open shoulders and deep V would enhance her figure. Inside a card stated, "I can't wait to be with you in every way."

No one. Not her deceased husband, an ex-boyfriend, or anyone else ever surprised her with a gift "just because." She normally did the surprising. Making sure people were taken care of fell on her. No one had ever done things to make sure she was good.

The physical connection between her and Dallas proved to be outstanding. But this ... this brought tears to her eyes. Looking at her cell phone, she realized she might still catch him before his plane took off. Quickly dialing, she gushed, "It's beautiful."

Laughing Dallas replied, "I take it you got the box."

"I have both of them," she exclaimed.

Dallas paused a few moments too long, "I only sent one."

And in that moment, she froze.

Chapter 4

Dallas broke every speed limit in Texas trying to get to Alicia. Something in her tone when they discussed the "other" package worried him. Desperation broke the normal strength of his voice. "Alicia!?

"Babe!" Alicia launched from the bed wrapping her thighs around his waist. "I wasn't expecting you for at least another half hour."

His world righted again. Crazy how something as simple as an embrace could wash away the silt of anxiety.

"Well, I made the team let me off the plane first." Laughing, he added, "They all think I've lost it. No doubt I'm going to hear about that tomorrow."

"You didn't have to rush. I told you I'd be here." She leaned back as though trying to read his eyes.

"No, I did have to rush." He disagreed as he guided her head against his chest. "You were too far away from me."

Her body's scent unfurled his anxiety. Her heartbeat paced with his, and the softness of her lips against his burst a damn of emotion within him. People talk about catching feelings like a cold in winter. And now, with Alicia in his arms, he realized he might have joined their ranks.

Dallas sat in the armchair, cradling Alicia in his lap. "I'll take the jokes and side comments. All of them are nothing compared to an extra second by your side."

"Well," Alicia smiled, though he'd seen her eyes brighter. "Since you're here and this bed hasn't gotten a good workout, why don't we?" Her eyebrows rose up and down quickly as she nodded towards the bed trying to entice him for a little time between the sheets.

Dallas jumped up from the chair as if a hot poker had been shoved where the sun didn't shine, almost dumping her on the floor. "Nope. We have plans. Where is my box?"

Alicia's eyes refused to meet his. Settling somewhere along the bridge of his nose.

Pulling her back towards him, he realized cracking the trust walls may require a larger hammer than he currently commanded. "Baby, what was in the second box?"

Her eyes brightened. A bit too much. "No, sir. I want my surprise. What are we going to do? Go out?" Her fingers crawled up his arm. "Stay in?"

He saw through her attempted topic change as easily as he picked apart screens on the basketball court. Dallas ran his hand through her hair and massaged the back of her neck.

Watching her eyes close as she leaned into his touch, he knew this wasn't the time. He could push and potentially derail the whole evening or let her slide until he could come at this from a different angle. Choosing the latter, he kissed her forehead, grabbed the box and her hand.

"Come with me." Her hand relaxed in his.

They took the elevator down to the lobby and a separate elevator to the Club Suite where he had a room.

He'd thought for sure this is where she'd be when he was out of town. Yet, she insisted on retaining her own room under the impression that she'd be more comfortable. How could she not be comfortable in a suite at the Ritz Carlton? It's like saying, no I don't want your temper-posture-massaging-coil-pedic mattress, I have this sleeping bag from my junior high camping trip that I can use instead. Made no sense.

While Dallas felt their growing attraction, trust eluded them still. He understood. A professional athlete's life isn't easy. Even weeding through women's intent often required surgical precision. Some athletes whored around. No doubt. A man didn't have to be a professional athlete to cheat. Any more than a man with a 9-5 job would always be faithful. Men did what they were going to do. Cheating was a choice. Being faithful was his only option.

Alicia planned. She watched her investments like a hawk ensuring she stayed within her means. That gave her the flexibility to be a nomad, to pick up and leave whenever she deemed fit. But he felt something else was the driving force behind her desire not to stay in one place too long.

He needed to prove to her that she could plant roots with him. He'd love to stay in Dallas, but the life of a professional athlete rarely ever aligned. He knew he could always be traded if a lucrative deal emerged. Maybe if he could show Alicia what life could be like with him, between them, she would stay.

Dallas felt her desire. The way her eyes lit up when theirs connected. The way she weaved her fingers through his when they watched television. Even the pillow fight when they played King of the Mountain. He changed the rules making it more of an adult game until she declared him King when she screamed through her orgasm. Only in basketball did he play by the rules, everywhere else, he pressed his advantage.

As they entered his suite, the glam squad he had the concierge arrange were waiting in black smocks and tools of their trade lined the table.

Alicia stopped at the door. "Wait. What?"

Dallas placed his finger over her lips. "Get ready. And for the record, they have no clue what's happening. So pumping them for information would be futile."

He watched her saunter into the room with the makeup artist, hairdresser, and stylist that purchased the dress. He turned towards the office where his suit for the evening hung pressed and ready to go.

On the desk sat a small box with a card tented on the top. In Alicia's handwriting, it stated, *"In case you need something to be mesmerized by."*

Inside lay a gold pocket watch on a chain. Laughter erupted as he shook his head. That's his Alicia. Earlier, he had compared her hips to the pocket watch of a hypnotist. She remembered and surprised him. Constantly, her humor, small observations, and just plain wit kept him engaged.

Looking at his new watch, he knew she'd be in hair and makeup for at least an hour. His spine tingled with the feeling of something being off about that second box and her expression when he asked about it. He had time. So, he rushed back to the elevator that would take him to her room. Yet, when he scoured the place it didn't appear to be anywhere. Where in the world would she put it? Glancing around again, he found her phone lying on the table like a time-bomb that would explode regardless of what he did.

His mental decision matrix shifted to determined. He recalled the code she carelessly typed all day to access her phone. Each number he punched irritated his sense of right and wrong. If not for the shadow under her eyes, the strain of her smile, and that she wouldn't lock eyes with his, he'd wait her out. Opening the phone, he noticed only one outgoing message to a Detective Faraday containing a photo with a note. "The original is on its way."

Slumping in the desk chair, Dallas realized he put himself in an even worse position. Who the fuck was Taric? Why the hell did she need a Chicago Detective? Why in the world was Dallas not far enough?

The tension he felt her release earlier crawled up his back and settled in his shoulders. No answer. More questions. Dallas sure as hell couldn't ask Alicia. He had hacked her phone. No woman, no matter the relationship status, believed it was okay for the guy they're dating to randomly scroll their cell. Hell, he knew while he punched in the code that it wasn't okay.

Yet, here they were. That first night. The night of the auction. He thwarted her original plan to leave on the red eye. He thought her antsy feet were running to something. Could it also be possible she was running away? Time continued to pass as he pulled out her desk chair and sat while he decided on his next step. He dialed out on his cell phone. In for a penny ....

"Kent, man, I need a favor."

Chapter 5

Alicia stared at herself in the full-length mirror in the closet of the Club Suite. She walked forward and backed away trying to see herself from every angle. Damn, she looked good. She never had problems finding men to date before. She knew how to work with what she had. However, after seeing the fairy dust the professionals sprinkled on her, she realized, there was a whole other level.

The dress with the sequins, open shoulders, deep neck, and cinched waist, put everyone on notice, stand back, real curves coming through.

Her hair always responded better to a third party than it ever did under her own hand. However, the hairstylist added additional tracks to her already long and thick hair giving her the ability to throw it around. Her hair alone screamed *toss me, tug me, I'm yours*.

Her reflection drew her closer to the mirror admiring the makeup artist's handiwork. Her eyes appeared more seductive, her cheeks contoured within an inch of their life, and her lips popped and glistened. Turning her head to the left and right admiring their work, Alicia's smile brightened at her transformation. This is red carpet ready.

A small knock on the door awoke Alicia from her fixation. The glam squad left first closing the door behind them, allowing her to make an entrance. Taking a deep breath, she opened both doors and walked through.

As much as she wanted to believe Dallas' words, "You are stunning," Alicia knew guys said random things all the time. But staring in Dallas' eyes, the way they remained transfixed on hers as he took steps forward, the small smile, he might not be aware of, graced his lips. Warm desire rolled off Dallas and wrapped itself around her shoulders.

Smiling, they clasped hands and navigated the hotel until they reached the doors leading to the pool.

Alicia paused with apprehension. "I'm not dressed for a dip in the pool." All the effort the team put in wouldn't be in vain. Someone would see her epic flyness, and it wouldn't be the pool guy.

Laughing, Dallas agreed. "Neither am I." Leaning over, he teased. "But there is always your birthday suit."

Hitting his arm and turning to see if anyone paid attention, "Be good."

"Good? If your nightly screams are any indication, good is too low of a bar."

Alicia glared, though she knew it didn't hold any heat. He didn't lie.

When they walked through the threshold of the door, the beauty of the pool area assaulted Alicia's eyes. She didn't know where to focus. A golden platform rose from the center of the pool. A two-person table with clear chairs and a table sat atop. On one side of the edge of the pool, a purple Mystical rose wall stood, initials D & A embedded. Although the sun remained high in the sky, they were situated in a way that if they turned to the left they'd see the rose wall. If they turned to the right, they'd view the sunset.

The music from a live jazz quartet wafted onto the deck.

Words and the ability to walk left as she just tried to take in the scene before her.

Dallas created this for her. For them. Every time she turned some other detail caught her eyes.

"Well …" His question hung between them. Alicia's emotions ran about like a herd of cats. A man who could put this together remained single? It didn't make any logical sense.

"This isn't a Wednesday night decoration. This is a wedding night decoration. "Why?" Alicia's mind resisted the emotions that she dared not name.

Dallas composed his thoughts before asking, "Remember when we argued about Abraham Lincoln?"

Alicia nodded.

"Or when my stomach cramped from laughing so hard that I begged you to stop laughing, and you couldn't."

"Yes, you ended up on the floor, which made me laugh even more."

"Right," Dallas explained. "You make me think. You make me laugh. You make me excited." He laughed before continuing. "You're stubborn as hell. Think you're right all the time. And I don't doubt could probably drive me insane with your control issues. But, we work so well. From day one."

Alicia squeezed his hand. As crazy as it sounded, they connected the minute their eyes first met.

"This," Dallas pointed at the amazing display. "is light work. If the biggest problem I have is how to show you what you mean to me and what we could be together, challenge accepted."

A waiter appeared offering two flutes of champagne.

"I don't need all of this. I'm enjoying becoming closer to you."

Dallas placed one finger over her lips. "Why is everything about you? The wonder that I see in your eyes. The way your head is turning to take in every little detail. The smile that has yet to leave your face. I need that. That makes me whole."

Alicia couldn't stop her lips from smiling or her heart from opening even broader. "Oh my god. You are so needy."

As he jerked her up towards the pool, she screamed. Laughing, he pulled her into his embrace and gently rocked with her.

"So," she said. "Just to be clear. This fantasy is for me?"

Dallas stopped; brow furrowed in confusion. "Yes."

"Good. Take off that suit jacket, mister. My hands are itching for your abs."

Laughing, he replied. "This is Tom Ford."

"In my shoes, he might request the same thing," she reasoned as her memory recreated what she knew lay underneath. "The shirt can stay on. Just unbuttoned."

Dallas balked just a bit. "I can't believe this."

"You have created a visual masterpiece." She licked her lips because just the thought of her man's body moistened everything. "I want to fully experience it."

Dallas grabbed his belt. "Oh, you want the full—"

"Not *that* full." She nodded to the musicians.

"Abs are enough for now." She chuckled. "I can be patient. Plus, I want to experience this. It's like my heart is nestled in the softest cotton."

"You are so precious. Why hasn't anyone made you feel this way?"

Unraveling the complicated layers of her life with her ex-husband would take a while and shouldn't intrude on this night. Now, she just wanted to feel, as she soaked in the happiness. She didn't remember the last time she was happy. Removed from the family drama, and the marriage that didn't live up to its expectation, this was too good. It wasn't meant to last, but who cared about tomorrow? She leaned in and placed her head on Dallas" bare chest. Kissing it softly while wondering what he'd planned for dessert.

Chapter 6

Kent King met Dallas at the door of the stadium as he arrived for practice. "Walk with me," he demanded.

As usual, Kent didn't waste words. Kent matched Dallas in height and stride. As a former professional basketball player turned police officer, he led the basketball franchise's security, and he knew what it took to protect the team. He handled all details needed for the security team to run efficiently, including doing a monthly check to make sure team members didn't lose their license due to unpaid tickets. Most importantly, Kent never talked out of school. Nothing told to Kent in confidence ended up in a tabloid or even a locker room rumor. Kent ran a tight ship and demanded that all security who worked for him develop a case of short-term memory loss.

Kent's office stood as a shrine to basketball. The players not only respected him but often left him signature items just because. Kent plopped in his chair while pulling a file from his drawer. "You wanted background on Taric Hasan and Alicia Mitchell?"

Nodding, Dallas braced himself for whatever caused Kent's jaw to clench.

"Well, Detective Faraday is a homicide detective in Chicago."

Dallas clutched the arm of the chair tighter. "Continue."

Kent flipped a page. "According to the police report, Alicia met Taric online, they dated. He told her he renovated buildings for a living. She drove past one of his buildings unannounced and went inside to see if he was there. Allegedly, at the time, he stood over another woman who was tied to a table. Alicia got the hell out of dodge. By the time the police arrived, Taric was gone. The woman left dead. Alicia remains a witness to the crime. And from the looks of it, she's the only witness."

"Damn." Dallas rubbed his forehead. Alicia was tied up with a psycho killer. "And?"

Kent flipped a few pages. "That's it. Taric—that's not his real name by the way—disappeared into thin air. Poof. Gone." Kent's expression didn't change. "How do you fit into all of this?"

Dallas stood and peered out of the window that looked onto a concrete hallway. "I'm seeing someone new. Alicia."

Kent leaned back into his high-backed office chair. "Figured as much."

"We spent the night at the Ritz. Taric contacted her there."

"Shit," Kent muttered, scratching his head. "Did she tell Detective Faraday?"

Dallas drummed his fingers against the window frame. "She told him. The person she didn't tell, any of this to, is me."

"Well, in her defense, when do you bring a killer into a conversation?" Kent pulled at his beard. "She needs protection."

Dallas released a low throaty chuckle. "Right. How can I arrange for protection if I'm not even supposed to know she needs protecting?"

Kent twisted his wedding ring in circles around his long finger. "Listen, that's why my job isn't always easy. I'm often required to pry the truth, no matter how embarrassing or detrimental to their careers, from millionaires who would rather keep their lives private. Never mind that social media makes that impossible." Kent shrugged. "They still try."

Dallas thought that over, then formed a plan. "Maybe you could talk to her."

"Not likely. She appears fiercely independent. Those types don't like restrictions. And girlfriends aren't in my job description unless they pose a security threat." Kent's smile lowered to a smirk. "If she didn't tell you, how did you find out about Taric?"

Dallas slouched into the chair with his shoulders by his ears. "It's possible her phone accidentally turned on while she was indisposed."

Kent held up his hands in defeat. "I'm out. You need to talk to her, though. This is serious. Is she coming to the game? I can let security here know. Alert the police."

"No need," Dallas assured, sliding the file from Kent's desk into his hands. "For good reason, she prefers watching the game on television."

Kent stared at Dallas with his head tilted to the side. "While I can appreciate the predicament, it puts you in an unwinnable position. As Taric isn't a direct threat to you, there isn't a lot I can do about it."

A plan formed behind Kent's dark brown eyes. "What?" Dallas enquired.

Kent leaned forward clasping his hands on the desk. "The easiest plan of action may be to cut ties with Alicia. A killer is more baggage than is needed for the first date. With your high-profile lifestyle, it's only a matter of time before your … um … association gets out."

"Not an option." Dallas leaned forward, focusing on nothing in particular. "She is an unexpected pleasure that I can't let go."

"Come on," Kent interjected. "There are more … many more women that you can date. I see them at parties, in the stands. All brightened and tightened, hoping for you to notice."

"Yeah, I can't bring any of that home to my mother." His mother would literally chop him off at the kneecaps if he brought any one of the NBA groupies to sit at her dinner table.

Kent folded his hands on his desk. "And you're planning on bringing Alicia home?"

Dallas intentionally didn't answer. The answer for him wasn't if, but when. For Alicia, who knows?

"So . . ." Dallas put his elbows on his knees staring intently at Kent. "What do I do?"

Chapter 1

"Stay," Dallas whispered in her ear.

Alicia stretched against him before settling into his arms. "Where am I going? My legs are still shaking with exhaustion."

"Yeah, sure. *That's* why they're shaking," Dallas countered with a laugh that rumbled in his chest.

He did have a point. His talent didn't just lie on the basketball court. She almost gave herself a high five for embarking on this particular journey. "Whatever." Alicia's eyes and her mind drifted as she welcomed sleep.

"No, I mean move out of the hotel and stay at my condo, with me."

Those words snatched sleep from Alicia faster than being doused by bucket of cold water. Playing it cool to try to tamp down on the fear bubbling in the background, she pretended that her mind wasn't screaming, *Ruuunnn*. Throwing in a yawn for good measure, she snuggled deeper before adding, "And leave all this." She relaxed and regulated her breathing allowing him to believe she'd fallen asleep again.

She laid still until his rhythmic breathing indicated he'd succumbed to fatigue. Extracting herself from his hold, she then snuck out into the kitchenette, hands shaking, she grabbed a bottle of water before settling on the couch. She didn't open it. Instead, her hands clutched it as she rocked back and forth.

Releasing the fear, Alicia attempted to think logically. Dallas *wasn't* Taric. He *wasn't* Taric. Chanting that in her head, the shaking receded.

A part of her wanted to give Dallas the peace sign and head to her next adventure. Fear controlled that part. Fear didn't belong in her relationship. In any relationship, though it sat beside her, eating a sandwich and smacking, and whispering, *girl I wouldn't do that if I were you*.

If Taric wasn't still a specter in her life, Alicia would've packed her bags. Her sense of adventure so long denied said *go for it*. Just as quickly, her brain would flash to that room, the crinkling of the plastic, the woman laying prone on the table.

Although she swore she had fallen asleep on the couch, she woke up stretching in the bed. On the nightstand next to her lay a key and a note. "*If your legs feel stronger today.*"

She ambled down to her room to think without the reminders of Dallas in every corner. That man did know how to make memories. Damn good ones. She opened the door to her room to retrieve her phone and paused. Her brain may have been scrambled last night, but she knew where she left her phone. It wasn't on the desk by the chair. Housekeeping? Maybe. Yet her towels lay on the floor along with the bathroom notecard request.

Carefully moving around, nothing else appeared out of order. Could Taric have been in her room? Possibly. Nothing in the space connected her to Dallas. Not even her phone. She had old school memorized his number to secure their privacy. The only connection would be the hotel staff.

At the Ritz, could he bribe someone? Throwing her clothes in a suitcase, Alicia scrambled to remove herself from the hotel as quickly as possible. Next, she went to her mobile phone dealer to get a new phone and number. After spending a couple of hours at a coffee house to both kill time and make sure she wasn't followed, she hopped in her rental car and called Detective Faraday.

"Faraday," his gruff voice responded. The first time she'd spoken to Faraday he had the weary voice of someone putting in time until retirement. Yet when she met him in person, his well-kept thirty-something body, and eyes sharp enough to catch changes in someone's pulse rate belied his beleaguered voice.

"Hi, it's Alicia. I have a new number. Anything on Taric?"

Faraday paused. She heard the creak in his chair that meant he'd adjusted to give her his undivided attention. Same sound whether he was on the phone or in person. "Alicia. Hey." He spit out what she assumed were the sunflower seeds he kept as a constant snack. "I haven't even found a viable alias. He's in the wind. But, I've notified the Dallas police. How long are you going to be there? Thought you were headed out of the country."

Alicia thought about her evening. "I was. I became distracted."

Silence met that statement.

Life might have been easier if she had left the country. Would Taric fly overseas to track her down? Less likely. "I know I should."

"I didn't say a word," he quipped. "It's not my business. I just remember you got caught up with Taric as a *distraction*. Something to do. So, be careful."

Faraday didn't lie. She planned to just enjoy life. So long term relationships didn't fall within her vision of the future. Taric's online profile displayed a beautiful man with a fit body that shouted swipe right. His job description included physical trainer and home flipper. Someone who managed his own time. Perfect.

He knew how to pick wine and make her laugh. She wanted easy.

Taric proved easier than a hooker on the stroll. After the first date, he became all about the sex, as if a bottle of wine the night before was the price of admission to intimacy.

Physically, she wasn't there. No ringing bells, no imagining him naked. Just a nice date. She took a hard pass when he suggested that she meet him at a building he was in the process of rehabbing.

That decision might have saved her life.

To describe Dallas with the same term as Taric didn't do him justice. "Very true. Let's say in this case he's not a distraction; he's a compulsion."

"Interesting," Faraday acknowledged, with a hint of skepticism. "I dated my fair share of forgettable women. Then I met my wife, Sarah. When my own mother told me to shut up about her unless she showed up at a family dinner, I figured she was different. So, I get it."

"Well," Alicia admitted. "I did the marriage thing. Done with that. But, this feels good."

"It would have to be to shift your whole travel the world perspective," Faraday agreed, then cleared his throat. "But still. Be careful."

"Got it. What are the next steps regarding Taric?" Alicia inquired.

"We have the box and note. Our analysts are going over it with a fine-tooth comb for clues. Outside of that, we must wait for him to emerge again. The good thing is you're in a different state. Hopefully outside of his comfort zone. Force him to make a mistake."

This was her life. "I wasn't aware that luck was an official investigative technique."

Faraday responded, completely unoffended. "Luck. Voodoo. Ouija board. Whatever works. I work the case and follow up on any viable lead until Taric is in jail. And I'm confident that he will end up behind bars. His ego is in it now. He could have left you alone. He didn't. That will be his downfall."

"How can you be convinced?" Her body shuddered in fear, not absorbing the warmth of his confidence. "You have nothing to go on."

"I have me." Faraday continued, "I was watching this show about wide receivers in the NFL. How they must believe they are the best in the league. They need to be ready to excel on every play. No one else can live in their head. If so, they won't be the best. Same for me. I'm good at what I do. My track record proves it. And I will catch the son of a bitch who killed that woman and who's harassing you."

"Whatever it takes," Alicia restated.

"Exactly."

"What if it takes my death?"

Chapter 8

Dallas stood by the door with a cocktail in one hand and a blindfold in another. As Alicia tentatively stepped in, he gave a smile that would normally have lifted her spirit by ten.

Instead, she frowned, pointing to the apron he wore, she asked, "Did you cook dinner?"

Laughing he admitted, "No. That's not hot or sexy for anyone." He pointed at her, noting the one carryon bag in her arm. "Is this all of your luggage?"

"No," she replied. "The rest are in the rental car waiting for those NBA muscles to bring them in."

"Did you cancel your room at the Ritz?" he inquired.

Eyes shifting to the side, Alicia responded, "Not yet."

"Hmm," Dallas nodded, "We'll, get to that later." Holding up the blindfold he asked. "Do you trust me?"

Alicia stared at him. He had no clue what she saw, but she agreed. "Yes."

He handed her a drink before tying the blindfold around her head. "We are only going into the dining room. It's on this floor with no floor level changes. I'll move you if you're about to walk into the door."

Alicia brushed her finger along the glass until she found the rim. Working slowly, she sipped on the drink. "Ohhh, delicious."

"I can't cook," Dallas admitted. "But I can make a mean drink."

"Noted."

Dallas placed her hand in the crook of his arm. As they slowly made their way past the kitchen to the dining room, he shared. "This morning, I woke up and thought. *How can I make today special for Alicia?*" Dallas paused and lifted the drink from Alicia's hand and placed it on the table. "That's new for me."

"Why," she inquired. "Do you discard women that often?"

Dallas didn't hesitate. "Maybe. Or maybe I don't really care if they stay or go. With you." He pulled the chair out and guided her in front of it before sitting her tight to the table. "With you, I want to make memories."

"All riiight," Alicia said, drawing out the word, but not providing any commentary on what she wanted other than alcohol. "Where is that drink again?"

Dallas placed her hand on the stem of the glass allowing her to manage to get another sip. In the meantime, he walked away to get the first plate. Alicia hadn't moved, tried to peek, or anything.

Alicia took a long whiff of the air. "I smell vanilla?"

"Yep," Dallas agreed. "Vanilla scented candles."

"I thought you said you didn't invite women to your house."

"I don't." Dallas threw up his hands. "I might have had help from someone else in putting this together."

"An ex?" Alicia inquired pulling her neck back as she shot him a crazy look even through the blindfold.

"No, my agent." Dallas chuckled. "Exceptional negotiator and fabulous taste in candles."

"Well, I—"

Before Alicia could get any idea, he added. "And married. Happily. Nothing to see there."

With a sheepish grin, she confirmed. "Got it."

He gently rubbed her head. "So tonight, I want to feed you."

"But not your cooking?" Alicia confirmed. Clearly. she had no faith in his culinary skills. With only a few anecdotal stories, and not any actual evidence.

However, he comforted her. "Absolutely not my cooking."

Dallas took a spoonful of Avocado Shrimp Risotto. "Open wide." He slid it into her mouth.

His tongue wanted to follow, but he held strong. "Any idea what you're tasting?"

After a bit, Alicia identified, "Heaven. Shrimp, Avocado. Olive Oil?"

"Wow, you taste olive oil?" Tilting her head from side to side as if still trying to get a feel for the food, Alicia admitted, "I use a lot of olive oil when I'm not deep frying. So, it would be my go-to guess."

"Fair enough. How does it feel on your tongue?"

"Not as good as you." She acknowledged with a cheeky grin. His dick throbbed in response. "Hearty. Creamy. If it wasn't for the shrimp, I might not have to chew. This isn't rice, though. I know it isn't rice. Polenta, quinoa? No quinoa is smaller."

"Anything else." He prodded.

"The warmth of it going down. Filling."

"Ok." Open your mouth again. As she opened her mouth, he placed another item along her teeth. "Bite down."

Once again, she opened and complied. "Hmm, chocolate-covered strawberries."

"Yes, dark chocolate to be exact. I have extra for later."

Her nipples hardened through the shirt, and her body squirmed just a bit. Her tongue shot out of the corner of her mouth, and the tip wet her lips. "Why wait?"

Alicia's tongue could only be described as the eighth wonder of the world. Every time she bit into food, her tongue would rim her mouth to ensure it gathered every bit of the tasty morsel.

Dallas couldn't restrain himself. He needed just a taste to tide him over. So, he bent over and joined his lips to hers. A fire erupted in him, and he let it rise. He curbed the instinct to rip off the blindfold and the buttons on her shirt keeping those lush breasts hidden from his view. The game was the sweetest torture he could have imagined. But, he wanted it to end. He didn't lie when he said he wanted to make memories.

He pulled back, admiring her slightly open mouth inviting him for another taste. Instead, he fed her a bite of the entrée. "What's this?"

"Oh, lamb." She chewed, and even the basic act of food consumption became sensual. "Really good lamb. I should get a prize for every taste I get right."

Chuckling, he inquired, "What kind of prize?"

"A kiss."

Another thing that set her apart from women in the past. She didn't ask for a piece of jewelry, a car, or cash. A kiss. Something he planned to hand over freely.

Leaning over to whisper, he proposed. "Tell you what. Why don't we do it this way? I'll give you points now that you can redeem in the bedroom later."

She settled back into the chair. "Sold. What's next?"

Alicia's phone vibrated.

A text message appeared,. *Hey Suga. Pick up for me.*

Dallas bit out a curse.

Immediately, she demanded to know, "What? Who is it?"

Sighing in frustration, Dallas unwrapped the blindfold. *The woman just changed her number today. How is this even possible?*

"Dallas?" Fear laced her voice as she ripped off the material and stared at the message.

Taric Hasan. Her phone rang.

He found her. Again.

Chapter 9

Reality burst the tension, building with each bite. Alicia picked up the phone.

Her eyes focused on Dallas as she whispered, "Hello," and clicked to record the call.

"Hey, Suga."

Like her dream almost two nights before. His darkness rose, throwing a shadow on her future.

She'd worried since that dream that she would be drawn to his southern drawl like a bee to honey. That something in her must desire the monster in him. Now, hearing it when consciousness reigned, his voice washed over her like a sports drink over the head of the winning coach, leaving her shaken to the core.

That second's long respite disappeared as she realized Taric Hasan's voice reached through her new cell phone.

"Taric." What else could she do, but acknowledge his existence?

She broke contact with Dallas" gaze, not wanting him to see the emotions flitting across her face. Pushing back the chair, she started to rise to leave the room until he placed a hand on her shoulder, holding her still. She remained seated. "Just itching to find your way to a jail cell, aren't you?"

Laughing, Taric responded, "I missed your strength. My last, um, friend didn't pose as much of a challenge."

The last friend. "You mean the woman I saw?"

"No, Suga'," he said with a disdainful laugh. "She wasn't the last."

According to Detective Faraday, aspects of Taric's M.O. were unique. They felt he must have been new to the scene. Even if that was true, that didn't mean he'd remain new.

"The moment you stepped onto that tarp," he continued. "I mean if you could have seen your face. The surprise and fear registered, but split seconds after the resolution. No freezing in horror for you. You barely blinked before you sprinted out of there faster than my knife slicing through skin. Unfortunately, I couldn't chase you. As you saw, Cecily demanded my attention."

"You. Killed. Her."

"I dream of you." He continued. His menace-laced voice would make the devil watch his back. "Your eyes from that day. Your body trembling, trying to adjust to the levels of adrenaline coursing through your body. Your scream as my knife made its first incision."

Dallas tensed; his breathing provided the soundtrack for the call. His brows knit, and his fist clenched and unclenched. Alicia closed her eyes; she needed to focus. Their one shot at catching him remained with her. One word. Just one might make the difference. Save his next victim. Save . . . her.

"I've been looking for another like you. A fighter. They keep offering me things. Before, and definitely after, I get started. Always. Before we even date. Cash. Their body. One lady offered me a trip on our first phone conversation."

"Really," Alicia countered. "What was her name?"

"Cute." He chuckled. Alicia listened to background noise over the phone. Hoping for the same luck she'd mocked Detective Faraday about. The luck that would lead to a clue that would lead to Taric. "Even now, your desire to catch me outweighs your fear of what you know I'll do to you. You of all people should be ruled by that fear. Especially given your history. Interesting."

Alicia continued to listen hard. No airplane, no next-door arguments. Did this man live in a bubble? Come on.

"They don't deny me as you did," Taric informed her. "Tell me. Why did you decide to come to the apartment that day?"

Alicia thought. "I don't know. Something told me to stop. Check it out."

"Ah. Intuition. That's so sexy." Taric chuckled before his voice dropped an octave, and he whispered. "My fingers still yearn for your flesh."

Fear caused her stomach to churn, but she refused to stop the conversation. The longer she talked the more chances she gave him to reveal something. She could only hope Taric cracked before she did.

"Aren't you afraid of getting caught," Alicia asked. "Afraid that coming for me will lead to you getting arrested."

"Fear doesn't serve any function in my life," he warned. "Either I'm going to do something or I'm not. I could die driving over to Central. Or I could live to be one hundred. It's all a roll of the dice. Wouldn't you agree?"

"I would agree that you could die any time. Yes." Alicia flickered a gaze to Dallas who stood as if he wanted to snatch the phone from her. She held up her hand to stop his progress. "What name would they put on your tombstone?"

"Mine is irrelevant. I'm more concerned about what they're going to put on yours. Don't worry, though. I'll be sure to attend your services.

Support your friends in their time of need. It will be my pleasure. Yes, after I'm done with you, I'll relish wrapping my arms around someone you hold dear."

With that, he disconnected.

Alicia's body trembled as she ended the recording to send a copy to Detective Faraday. He'd call as soon as he heard it. Until then, her body trembled so hard that even Dallas" strong arms couldn't absorb it. She should take a shot of something. Anything. As if reading her mind, Dallas brought over a glass of Makers Mark.

Even then, she couldn't relax. Her mind worked on a problem. Something she'd missed. Something she needed to figure out.

Pulling back, she realized what sent warning signals to her brain. "You know about Taric." She let that accusation hang between them. "From the time his number pulled up on caller ID to now, you responded as if I'd told you about him. But I didn't."

Before he could explain, she pushed him away and created distance between them. "Stay away from me."

Chapter 10

Pleasure and pain so closely aligned that the shift could be almost imperceptible. The fear emitting from Alicia's eyes sliced through Dallas like a dagger.

Dallas held up his hand. "No, wait. Give me one second." He quickly went into the kitchen to grab the file he'd basically memorized.

"The second package. The one you didn't tell me about. I needed to know." Taking a deep breath, Dallas tried to put his words together in a way that didn't fracture their strained understanding of each other.

"It's hard to know who to trust. And I can't let my emotions cloud common sense. Well, any more than I already have. Our first night together, I brought you back here. I never bring anyone to my condo. This is my sanctuary. I'm usually at the Ritz."

"Oh, *that's* why you get the five-star treatment there." Panic rose at the sound of her droll voice.

"That and I tip well." Interjecting a bit of comedy that Alicia had little time for, as indicated by her expression.

"Well and often?" She shot back.

"Don't push it. Listen." He reached for Alicia's hands, but she pulled away. "I did go to your room and open your phone. And saw the photos you sent to Detective Faraday. And sent them to Kent, head of security for my team. This is his report."

She froze. Her green eyes became pure ice. "You. You went to my room." She closed her eyes and began taking deep breaths; either she was trying to calm down or she was about to pop off. "I knew. Knew someone had been there. You scared me to death."

Alicia flipped through the first couple of pages of the report. Then quickly flipped through a few more pages. "Your basketball team knows about me," She shrieked.

Dallas didn't know if she posed a question or statement. "No, the organization doesn't get involved, but our head of security has to know if something is amiss."

"What security?" She snapped. "I haven't seen security."

"Security is best unseen. The charity event had security. They stayed in the background. The Ritz has security. The condo, of course, has security. I knew the minute you entered the garage. If you're in my life, people know about you. My agent helped me pull together last night and today. Mostly because she didn't trust me to coordinate all this myself."

"Listen." Dallas stepped back so she could see his face. "Kent is the best there is. I trust him. Literally with my life. Every day."

Tossing the report on the table, Alicia stated, "This file is basically about the original report I filed with the police."

"Yeah," Dallas agreed, then softly added. "Which is more than you've told me." He didn't want to push. He was already living at the door of the doghouse with her foot on his ass seconds from kicking him in.

Alicia dropped into the chair with her chin on her chest. "I should have told you. Especially after the box." Alicia motioned for Dallas to sit as well. "It all started with just one date that clearly didn't go well."

"And so now…" He leaned closer wanting desperately to have her in his arms, but he'd already crossed her boundaries once.

"Faraday will call soon. He'll want a breakdown of the conversation." Banging her hands against the table until the glass rattled, she added. "I don't like that Taric is this close."

"Neither do I," he agreed. Suddenly a thought came as to how to keep her protected. "Come to the game tomorrow night. At least I'd feel better if you're there."

"No, I'm not ready to go public just yet." Alicia rubbed her temple. Public meant exposure. And at this point, exposure could mean death.

"Come here, then." Dallas rose with his arms open for her to slide in.

Dinner forgotten. They went to the theater room and sat down on the sectional. Laying down with her face in his chest she delved deeper.

"Like I said. I wanted to have fun. Have company. I didn't need to spend hours figuring does he like me, where is this going, is he 'the one.' I just wanted to laugh. One of his photos pictured him by the lake with rollerblades. It looked like fun."

"And you stopped by the apartment because?" he hedged.

"He invited me there for date two at an apartment he was rehabbing. Empty apartment building? My friends said for sure that he was a serial killer. I laughed when they said it. I mean come on. I gave him married whore at best." The humorless chuckle underscored the incredible story. "After I declined, I was curious. I was in the neighborhood. And I passed by the apartment he was rehabbing. So I stopped and went in. The door wasn't locked, and I knew the owner, right? I thought a quick peek wouldn't hurt."

"And you saw him?" Dallas nudged.

"It was stuffy inside." Alicia's eyes stared into the distance. "Chicago summer needs air conditioning, but I guess it wasn't installed yet. I followed the whirring fans. The door was slightly ajar. My nightmares now have one of two elements. The crunch of my foot stepping on plastic or his voice saying, 'Hey Suga' in my ear. He always calls me Suga' with that southern drawl that is probably as fake as his name."

Alicia shifted. Dallas didn't want to interrupt so he wove his fingers through hers in an effort to offer comfort from this demon.

"It only took a second," she whispered. Even so, her voice caught as she took a second before continuing. "But the girl tied to the table didn't move. Blood dripped from her body. My eyes connected with Taric. And I ran the hell up out of there. Jumped in my car and sped off. Called 911 from the car."

Dallas kissed the top of her head.

"I hadn't heard from him at all. Not until the Ritz. He's still doing it. Still dating. Still killing. But apparently, I'm the challenge he didn't know he wanted."

"I'll call security to get someone on it," he offered. No way she would live unprotected. Not on his watch.

"This has nothing to do with your team. You play for them. I don't, and I don't want you involved in this mess." Alicia insisted.

"Is that why you were leaving on the red-eye the night I met you?" Dallas inquired, now wanting to figure out if she was running away from danger or towards some new adventure.

"Yes and no. I figured it wouldn't hurt, but that had been my plan all along. I want to see the world. Travel. Especially India. Marriage bound me to Chicago. I don't want to be tied like that again."

Dallas kissed her temple. "I can be your wingman."

Alicia sat up and turned to connect with his eyes.

"Not that kind of wingman. I'm not introducing you to any other man. But something about this fits. It's worth exploring. Anywhere in the world you are."

Alicia's only reply was a non-committal sound. They continued to lay there as sleep soon claimed their thoughts, words. Until desire invaded the nothingness of sleep. His hips found a rhythm before his brain could comprehend. His body knew to move, to drive forward without recognizing the why of the movement. His mouth opened, and his breathing shifted, as realization slowly crept into his consciousness. The scent of Alicia graced his senses. The warmth of her mouth against his most sensitive muscle caused desire to consume him.

Dallas reached down, splaying a hand over to her head, and he took over the rhythm of their movements. His body demanded more. Deeper. Harder. Until his consciousness and his body exploded in ecstasy.

As his panting calmed to normal breathing patterns, he opened his eyes to watch her looking up at him, smiling. Dallas pulled her up until he could overtake her mouth like she had invaded his senses. He wouldn't stop until he lived in her heart as she lived in his.

Completely.

Chapter 11

Alicia stood in the kitchen, elbow-deep in bubbles as she cleaned the dishes from the previous night. She needed something to do with her hands and since she had asked Dallas to cancel his normal cleaning crew, the chores fell on her. She didn't mind. Matter of fact, she used the same procedure to get through the night. Distraction.

Again, she'd jolted awake with fear snatching her breath away. She kept hearing Taric's voice in her head. She had two choices. Bang her head against the wall to drive it out or find another method. What's the point of dating the great Dallas Avery if she didn't allow him to be great?

Although she might need to discuss the terms and boundaries if this dalliance continued, she couldn't blame him though, those with a lot to lose had more to protect.

He thrust away all of her negative thoughts. She may have kicked things off with Dallas last night, but that man surely brought it on home. By the time they were on round two, she couldn't remember her name, much less anything else about her life. Alicia woke up whistling and baking homemade biscuits before reality tapped her on the shoulder and cleared its throat.

So this morning, she found herself leaning on a wet mop in the middle of the half-wet kitchen floor alternatively wondering where Taric was and what he knew, and then wondering how the hell Dallas knew how to do some of the things that made her tremble in broad daylight while he practiced with the team miles away.

Her cell phone rang. Brushing the suds on her pants, she answered as Faraday's number popped on the screen.

His gruff voice demanded, "Why didn't you call me instead of sending an email? And email is for dinner reservations, not evidence of serial murder."

Alicia shrugged, though Faraday couldn't see her. "The conversation ended. He hung up. It's not like you could trace it. Plus, it was late."

"Late or not, I could have had Detective Pierzynski follow-up," he snapped. "Listen, you're in danger."

"No shit." Alicia retorted. Faraday was talking like he's making a revelation. She'd been in danger since the day she stepped onto that tarp.

"No." Faraday paused, and seconds ticked by.

She hated when Faraday paused. That meant whatever was coming next was worse than whatever he said before.

"He's in Texas," he admitted. "Probably Dallas."

Alicia didn't know why her stomach suddenly dropped to her feet. A package did appear at the Ritz Carlton. Faraday's words stripped the comfort and security she'd gained at Dallas' condo. Now, standing in front of the window overlooking the city, she fought the urge to duck and crawl under the kitchen table.

"Alicia?" Faraday called to her. "Alicia!"

Sighing, she couldn't put her head in the sand and hope this went away. "What? What am I supposed to do?"

"I don't know if he knows where you are now but staying away from the Ritz might make him look for you."

"And if he finds me, he finds whoever I'm with?" Alicia realized even keeping Dallas under wraps couldn't guarantee his safety.

"Something like that." Faraday gulped something before she heard the cup hit the desk.

"Is that vodka? One of us should be drinking at this point." She'd have to find Dallas" stash. He did love a good whiskey.

"No. And neither of us should be drinking if we want to get Hasan."

"How did he find me? How could he—"

"You bought an NBA superstar at an auction. Not front-page news, but news nonetheless."

"Yeah." She admitted, hating the fact that helping a good cause put her back in the line of fire.

"And you stayed," Faraday added with censure deepening his tone.

Such a crazy game. If she'd left, Dallas might have been safe, but Taric might still have found her. "Right."

"So it's possible that if I'm not at the Ritz, he'll look for me. But if I do go to the Ritz, he has already found me." Alicia could drop into a deep hole and be absorbed into the Earth's magma. "What are my options?"

"Go back to the Ritz," Faraday suggested.

She couldn't have heard him right. "But—"

"No, buts. If you disappear so does he. And our best chance to catch him. He's not going to stop."

"Isn't that *your* problem?"

Martyr didn't have a line item on Alicia's resume. When she worked in corporate America for a brief stint she'd refused to be the floor monitor in case of a fire. Especially since everyone on the floor could hear the same fire alarm she did. If so, she wasn't checking offices for grown able-bodied adults, half of whom didn't even like her in the first place.

"I'd like to think of it as *our* problem. Especially since you met an NBA superstar and didn't leave."

She hated when Faraday shined a light on the problem when

the problem was her. True, if not for the auction, she'd be in India, meditating, centering herself, taking in a culture that had intrigued her since her teenage years.

Instead, she stayed. She couldn't say she regretted it. The past days had taught her more about what she wanted and needed than all the years of her marriage.

"Should I hire a security guard?" Alicia offered.

"You don't think the Dallas police can handle it? They can protect you. Now, you're amongst the elite, so run-of-the-mill police aren't good enough for you." Faraday sounded offended.

"Dallas offered and…" she added.

Faraday rustled some papers. "Call Pierzynski. Talk to him. It might give you clarity."

Alicia couldn't risk Dallas, and playing house put him in danger.

Chapter 12

Dallas paced the area in front of Kent's desk. "I have a bad feeling about this."

"About what? The game," Kent responded.

Dallas glared at Kent but refrained from letting loose with his first reaction which included a cell phone flying across the room at Kent's head. The front office frowned on staff assaults. It didn't matter who did it or for what reason. He couldn't let his team down.

"Alicia. I'd feel better if you could guard her," Dallas admitted.

"If I walked out of here to protect your brand spanking new girlfriend, both of us would be looking for new jobs. Wait." He amended. "*I'd* be jobless. You'd get a stern talking to. I could recommend someone."

Dallas waved him off. "I have recommendations coming out of my ass."

Kent nodded, but Dallas felt his eyes boring into him. "So I know for a fact that you enjoy the company of various women. Just keeping up with who you give your tickets to is a full-time job. What makes her different? Better yet, what makes her worth *my* job?"

Dallas stopped. He had never broken it down before. Didn't think too much of it. Why Alicia?

"I mean, she's more mature than you're used to," Kent continued.

"You mean *older*." Dallas felt the heat of anger rise.

Kent held his hand up in surrender. "I mean, more mature. Older, yes. But that's tabloid fodder. She's settled. Financially secure."

Dallas glared.

"No, don't ask me to find information on someone and don't think I'm not going to follow the money. I always follow the money. Best way to get to the bottom of motivations. This woman went to court trying to keep custody of her niece because the mother was unfit. She's stable. Smart. Isn't spending her last dollar on a party dress. She's different."

"Yes, she is." Thinking back to the auction, Dallas grinned. "I mean. The first night I met her she asked for an autograph, then tried to hand me off to one of the groupies circling the room. She honestly just wanted an autograph and to give to a good cause."

"Maybe she's a better actress than you've dealt with before," Kent offered, folding his hands and placing them on the desk.

"No," Dallas shook his head. "I think she's a better person." Dallas remembered the night before when she recorded the call. "She's brave and smart. And makes a kickass biscuit. Man, she made me want to call my mother and tell her to hang up her apron. Almost. I'm not that crazy though, man."

"Well, good to know that you haven't completely lost it," Kent agreed, giving him a lopsided grin. "Listen, the lead detective, Pierzynski, is good. Was on the force with him."

"What happened to Faraday?" Dallas inquired as that was the only name he knew.

Kent's eyebrows rose. "I suppose he's still occupying his skin in Chicago. We're in Texas. There is this thing called jurisdiction."

"Well, can you at least call her during the game to make sure she's all right? You know, rules and all. I just need to know she's good."

"Don't you have an assistant or something?" Kent queried, scowling.

"Kent, please." Dallas knew that he'd be a wreck unless he knew for sure that someone he trusted at least kept tabs on Alicia. Someone with connections to the police department.

"Fine. Give me the number," Kent grudgingly agreed.

Dallas transferring his anxiety into playing an aggressive game. He received a couple fouls that he normally wouldn't get, but other than that his defense kept his opponents scoring under control. The thumbs-up from Kent from the sidelines helped manage his concern. Until the fourth quarter, then Kent disappeared.

Forcing himself to focus, his team pulled out a win. Then, of course, he only spoke about two sentences to the media to fulfill his obligation before forcing them to part while he ran past the locker room with arena security hot on his heels.

He knew. The minute he peered into Kent's anxious eyes he knew.

"Somewhere between your condo and the Ritz, she disappeared."

Chapter 13

Closing her eyes, Alicia tried to listen to the sounds around her. Something that would reveal a location. Or where help would come from. Instead, her ears met the hollowness of stale air. Four concrete walls surrounded her. Industrial ceiling and concrete floor. Well, the underlying floor was concrete. When she turned her head, her gaze caught the corner of a blue tarp. *No. No. No.*

At one point, seeing a tarp just meant someone was about to paint. Life took a left turn. Now the tarp meant someone was about to die.

In Alicia's mind, the tarp meant Taric. That blue tarp from her nightmare. The tarp that had collected blood already, and now awaited hers.

Her memory didn't provide any clues on where Taric had taken her. As she turned her head the other way hoping for a clue to her salvation while knowing in the recesses of her soul that her life had ended the minute Taric kidnapped her.

Taric conducted his business in unmanned territories. As indicated by the fact, Alicia's bindings included her arms and legs while her mouth lay bare to scream. She did, pushing her voice to its limits until it cracked under the pressure. No one came.

The glint on the edge of the knife mocked her as she bucked against her restraints. Next to it lay a lighter normally reserved for charcoal at a barbecue. Both perfectly normal purchases, and yet together represented how casually Taric caused pain. Normalized torture. And continued his life with victims littering his past.

Alicia twisted left and then right searching for the littlest bit of give, none came.

Think. Think. She couldn't tell if her screams weren't loud enough or there wasn't anyone to hear. Yet, she didn't stop. She continued to tug. The ropes remained taut cutting into her wrists and ankles instead of loosening.

She shouted, hollered, and yelled to no avail. No one peeked their head in the door. And no one knew where she was.

Then the door opened. Her worst fears sprang like water from a dike.

"Did you miss me, Suga'?"

Chapter 14

What Dallas did after the game could be described as a shower only because water came from pipe affixed to the wall, but it was more like a run through. Dressed and back in the security office in less than ten minutes with his suit pants sticking to areas he hadn't dried correctly and his skin tightening without the lotion he normally applied, he wasn't even sure he'd swiped deodorant under each arm. And he didn't care.

Detective Alan Pierzynski proved to be the opposite of Kent. Having played professionally at one point before going into law enforcement, Kent kept his athletic physique trim. Pierzynski appeared as if he never met a meal he didn't eat. Slow and ambling, Dallas wondered how he caught anyone, much less murderers.

"Why did she go to the Ritz alone?" Pierzynski demanded. "Faraday told her to call me. She didn't."

"Listen," Dallas offered. "I'll get on television. How much of a reward do you need? I'll call my accountant. I'll do anything."

Pierzynski shook his head. "You'll do nothing."

Dallas couldn't have kept his legs from pushing him to his full height if they'd been injected with a sedative. "I won't take no for an answer."

"Well," Pierzynski barely registered Dallas' reaction with one eyebrow raised. "You will have to take no."

"Kent—"

"Just listen to him, man," Kent implored, sending a warning look to shut him down.

"Right now, the relationship is between Alicia and Taric. Right?" Pierzynski closed his eyes as if he planned to take a quick nap. "Any other element we add into the relationship makes it unstable. The last thing we want is a murderer to become even more unstable."

"Maybe if he knows the kind of scrutiny he'll get if he kills her, he'll back off," Dallas explained.

"That. Won't Matter. This. Is. Personal." Pierzynski enunciated each word as if by slowing his speech the situation would sink into Dallas' head. "He likes her. As crazy as it sounds, he respects her. He won't kill her easily or soon. He'll want to break her first."

"You got that from one recorded phone call?"

He opened one eye and gave Dallas a once-over. "Didn't you?"

Dallas paced and nervously playing with his cell phone, "All I got was he was crazy as hell."

"Going back to Alicia wasn't his first choice. He didn't like the desperation in other women. That tells us that he knows that Alicia is special, and he won't be able to replace her. So, he'll take his time."

Dallas collapsed back into the chair. "What is he going to do to her?"

"We don't know."

Dallas threw up his hands. "So, she's gone, and we know nothing."

Pierzynski's eyes popped back open. "Who said we didn't have anything?"

"You're taking a nap." Dallas tried hard not to grab Pierzynski by the collar and rattle him until he demonstrated even a modicum of the urgency the situation dictated. Alicia disappeared. Gone. Poof.

"My process. I'm reviewing evidence in my head and waiting for a call. He mentioned he could walk to Central. The grocery store. We can start showing pictures there."

"You know what he looks like?" Dallas turned to Kent. "That wasn't in his file."

Kent's eyes widened before an innocent countenance rested on his face.

Pierzynski merely shook his head. "Kent, handing over police files to civilians?"

"Most of the file. Enough to give information. Not enough to start his own investigation that could link back to me."

"Alicia downloaded his photo and sent it to one of her girlfriends along with everything she knew before her first date. Hell, we even know about the stolen license plates on the car he used to get to their first date."

"Can't you track Alicia's new phone?" Dallas enquired.

Pierzynski and Kent locked eyes before Pierzynski responded. "If it were on, we could. But …"

"But her phone isn't pinging off of any cell phone towers," Kent explained.

Suddenly Pierzynski shot up. Dallas jumped back while Pierzynski ran to the phone. "He's not just killing. He's dating. That's his pool. Someone else knows him." He shouted into the phone. "See if you can convince the online dating service to let us do a match on all the photos in their database, but only for the metro Dallas area."

Chapter 15

Taric wanted her strong and defiant. And since that's what he said he wanted; she would be the whiniest victim he'd ever met. Although it grated against her nature, she became the very type of victim that forced him to reach out to her.

She broke down into a big bold two-year-old when someone stole their candy. She added hiccups for effect. As she sniffled, she attempted to say a complete sentence. "Please," she begged. "I'll give you anything. My money. What do you want with me?" Alicia interjected a sob between each word with a wail at the end.

Taric's head cocked as he watched her, scowling, "I don't need you to give me money. It doesn't take much of a computer genius to wipe your account." Taric grinned. "I may have already."

"Mother—" Alicia growled. "Let me up from here. I swear I'll be the last woman you fuck with."

"What happened to the tears and the begging? That left really quick." Taric picked up her car key and jammed it into her hand.

The pain hit so suddenly that all her mouth could do was open before a noise she barely could comprehend ejected from her mouth.

"What do you feel? Do you want to offer me those delectable lips? Or do you want to curse me out? The truth now."

Alicia closed her lips. Her hand, no way to describe the pain pulsing from it. She thought she had a high threshold of pain. Nothing could prepare her for what she felt at the moment.

"The lesson to this is don't let the drawl fool you." He leaned over and whispered into her ear. "I'm not the one to be fucked with."

The tears streaming down her cheeks reflected the pain. But now more than ever, she promised herself she'd get out of this alive for no other reason than see Taric's homicidal manic ass behind bars.

Chapter 16

Pierzynski scratched his stomach. "Run up to Central," he murmured.
Kent sighed. "You're trying to go shopping while—?"
Pierzynski held up his hand. "Have you ever used the term 'run up to Central?"
Kent shrugged before responding, "Of course."
"Because …" Pierzynski nudged.
"Because I need food." Kent's head tilted slightly to the left as if he knew he had missed something, but not exactly sure what.
Pierzynski played an air piano. "Local people talk about local stores and landmarks a specific way. With a sense of familiarity. What if Taric didn't follow Alicia from Chicago?"

"What if he's been here and she came to him?" Dallas added. "She's in his playground. That makes it worse, right?"

Kent and Pierzynski shared another look. He didn't know who was supposed to translate it, but they knew something.

"If he's local, and remodels homes or apartment buildings . . .?" Pierzynski spoke his theory. "If he plays the same role he said he did in Chicago, then there is one place that may have seen him. And possibly remembered him because he's there often."

Kent and Pierzynski replied at the same time. "The permit office."

Pierzynski typed into his phone. "Let's get that picture down there. There, he would use his real name. He'd have to. There are rules. And hoops to jump through. And rules with hoops and hoops with more rules. And it helps if you have friends. He would absolutely have a friend in the permit office."

"People I know are waiting eight weeks for permits," Kent agreed. "Even contractors that submit their documents online are showing up in person to inquire. No way around it."

A sliver of light broke through Dallas" mind. "Would they know where he lives?"

"We don't need to know where he lives," Pierzynski responded. "We need to know where he works."

"They open at eight in the morning," Pierzynski rose and put his hand on Dallas' shoulder. "Go home. Get some sleep. Meet me at the precinct in the morning."

"No." Kent's voice expressed the finality of his opinion. "If we want to keep Dallas under wraps, that won't happen at the precinct. You know that as well as I do. The minute he walks through the door, the rags will be calling, trying to figure out why. He stays home." Kent turned to Dallas. "I'll be by in the morning. One of the other staff will be at the precinct keeping an eye on things. You won't be out of the loop, but you also won't be part of the story."

"That's it?" Dallas demanded. What if they were wrong and Taric killed Alicia tonight?

Pierzynski whipped out his cell phone. "No, but you should go home. Get some rest."

"Why?" Dallas whispered. Even he heard the crack in his voice though he tried to mask it by clearing his throat.

"I don't know what's going to happen tomorrow," Pierzynski explained. "Regardless, you're going to need all of your strength."

Dallas nodded before heading to the condo. Then, spent the evening ambling from room to room noting little signs of her presence though she never even officially unpacked. Alicia's electronic toothbrush.

She'd started imprinting herself on his life. He could lose her, that thought stole all vestiges of sleep.

Chapter 16

The quiet in the room unnerved Alicia. Time stretched like waiting for a pot to boil or a spin cycle to finish. She didn't know how long because there wasn't a clock on the wall or even a window so she could monitor the movement of the sun. Just artificial light and despair. Her despair.

She didn't know if she passed out or fell asleep. Most likely passed out as Taric bandaged her hand. It wasn't that he cared. He just wanted her around until he decided to end it. How long did he keep his women? How long did these nightmares last?

At least now she had peace; she didn't know for how long. A growing portion of her brain acknowledged she may not make it out alive, but she knew she'd fight with every last breath in her lungs.

When she closed her eyes, she forced her subconscious to bring up another memory to replace the manic bright eyes and the too-eager smile Taric displayed.

Dallas swam before her. She remembered the night before he left.

She was in the office typing when Dallas interrupted. He stood before her dressed in a tank top, black jeans with bare feet. He's home. He should be comfortable. The apron that he wore stopped her fingers mid-type.

"Why are you wearing an apron?"

Dallas already informed her that he couldn't cook. Not didn't, but couldn't. Unless she liked everything blackened and even then he referenced burning and not seasoning.

Dallas' lip pulled back into one of those smiles that made his eyes narrow, and her panties dampen.

He held out his hand. "Come."

Yes, please.

Alicia smelled the vanilla before her eyes feasted on the room. The candles provided a soft glow around the room. Soft jazz played in the background as he pulled her toward the massage table.

He lifted the edges of her white kimono and simply said, "Disrobe." He pulled it back before demanding again, "Disrobe."

She yanked off her shoes, pants, and top. "Happy?" She said as she made move to put her arm in the sleeve of the kimono. He pulled it back again.

"No. I'm not happy. Disrobe completely."

Now, she raised her eyes to his as she removed her bra. His eyes warmed as his gaze lowered to her breasts. His mouth opened slightly as he licked his lips. His gaze seared her making her want to take two steps forward but anticipating that may be against the rules.

"And?"

She bent over and slid the thong down her legs. Then watched his eyes again as she stepped out and kicked them back. His mouth opened as if he was going to consume a feast.

Neither moved until Alicia smirked. "Can I put on the kimono now?"

"No need," Dallas responded before tossing it aside. "Lay down."

Alicia complied, nestling her forehead on the donut-shaped pillow at the top of the massage table, grumbling, "Don't know why you have a robe if no one is going to be wearing it."

"What did you say?" He poured warm oil on her.

Sighing, she replied, "Nothing." Then he kneaded her shoulders, releasing the tightening running up her neck and threatening to become a full headache. "Nothing at all."

Alicia focused on the warm hands and oils caressing her body. Down the left side and back up the right before focusing again on her shoulders. Watching his legs, she lamented the fact that his waist was so high because all she wanted to do was suck on him like a pacifier.

Even as she raised her hand, he stepped back. "No. This is for you."

Something inside of her cracked. Maybe the shell around her heart. Maybe years of self-protection. Something.

As her body turned to gelatin and the only pain she could feel was the desire to be filled by him, he asked. "So where are you going to be tomorrow?"

"Jamaica," Alicia replied with a smirk.

To respond, Dallas rubbed her inner thigh. But he didn't touch her epicenter, though he had to feel it pulsating. Hell, he might see it throbbing, desperate for him. Now, she felt her body building, then sitting on the precipice of release. She couldn't stop the whimper that escaped her lips.

"Where are you going to be tomorrow?" he repeated, a smile lightening his words.

"Here. Here with you. Here," she panted.

"Good answer."

Dallas then plunged his fingers into her, and her body tightened around them sending her over the edge to an ecstasy that lifted her soul from her body. Her being fused back together, but instead of them heading off to the bedroom, Dallas stated, "Turn over."

Chapter 18

Alicia's gaze followed Taric around the room from the door to the table. She yearned to grab the scalpel that currently sat just out of reach and slice his hamstring, incapacitating him as he had done to her. Or maybe his Achilles tendon.

The vision of him tumbling to the ground brought on a smile. Even that wasn't enough. Not nearly.

She longed to make Taric scream in pain. Instead, he'd smirk at her, knowing he had the upper hand. For now.

Taric came back and brushed her forehead. "Suga, I love the way you watch me. Can't keep your eyes off me. All dark and foreboding as if you hate me. Do you hate me?"

Alicia glared until he tapped her injured hand. Then she threw out, "Yes," through clenched teeth.

"You didn't at one point in time," he taunted. "At one point, you flirted shamelessly."

This time, she merely shifted her gaze to her hand before she answered. "I didn't know you then."

"You don't know me now," Taric responded, trailing his hand down her arm. "I do need someone special in my life."

Alicia thought her ears played tricks on her. "Come again."

"I never lied about wanting a partner." He leaned and closer. "I have a gift for you. Remember your love of raincoats and matching umbrellas. You had them on our first date. So, I bought you …" He paused as he unwrapped his gift and showed her. "See. I pay attention."

"An umbrella? You bought me a yellow raincoat and an umbrella?" Even as the words left her mouth, she couldn't reconcile this reality. She lay, restrained. Her options were killing people or dying. His eyes remained hopeful that she'd actually choose to kill people. "Is that what you did for other women? Offer them gifts?"

"Oh god, no. Those whimpering, simpering," Taric shuddered as he placed the box on the table. "They would be a liability. You would be an asset."

"Except," she added. "I don't kill people. Not even for an umbrella."

"Except," he responded. "You'd kill me if you had a chance. Right? You'd take my life without a second thought. You'd lay me in a ditch and shovel garbage on my corpse."

Alicia couldn't deny it. Hell, she'd shovel garbage in his corpse if given the opportunity.

"So" he sneered. "Before you get all high on not being a killer. Maybe before you met me. Maybe even last week that would have been true. When I'm done," he explained leaning closer. "You might be my greatest triumph."

Alicia gathered her anger, frustration, and fear into a fist and struck out, connecting to Taric's balls. Hand pain exploded like a grenade.

Yet, as he crumpled to the floor, she added, "Or, you could be mine."

Chapter 19

Dallas could feel his heart pound so hard in his chest, almost as if it was trying to escape. His heart wasn't the one that needed escape. Alicia did.

The closest the police would allow him to the building was across the street and up the block. Even then, he remained in a car with tinted windows. Multiple agencies swarmed outside as Pierzynski reviewed the plans with other alphabet agencies to determine how they would proceed. If they swarmed, either they'd catch him, or he could simply kill Alicia. Dallas" leg bounced up and down as he tried to remain calm.

Kent sat beside him. "Are you sure you want to dive in this deep with someone you just met?"

Dallas turned and looked at Kent and paused before responding. "Yes, I'm sure."

There was a pause. A pause equaled a "but." "It's not too late for us to hightail it out of here. I get it. How could you possibly want to take on something like this one?"

"That is not what the pause meant." Dallas responded. "One, it's not her fault. Two, goodness knows you've kept some psycho stalker women at bay."

Dallas added, "And the third reason, and probably most important one is that I never thought to jet. I should have. I've left for less. That's probably the most confusing part. I didn't consider walking away from Alicia. I just know we aren't done. What can I say?"

"But," Kent persisted. "You don't know what's going to walk out that door. You have no clue what he's done to her."

Dallas couldn't explain his rationale in any other way but to say, "But I know who went in."

* * *

He knew the plan of attack already. The team reviewed the building plans provided by the permit's office. Thankfully, Taric, real name, Samael Brevil, had come to the permit's office once a week, religiously, for the past six weeks. He should have been there yesterday. He didn't show up.

Although hot outside, Dallas shivered. "Kent."

"Hmmm," Kent responded as he texted on his phone.

"You saw the full police report for the woman in Chicago. Did he … did he torture her? Mutilate her? Is that why you're asking? Is there something you're trying to prepare me for?"

Kent shook his head denying Dallas" train of thought. "We don't know what he'll do *or* won't do to Alicia. We'll have to wait and see."

Chapter 20

Alicia watched as Taric writhed on the cold concrete floor attempting to regain his breath and waiting for the pain to subside.

He hadn't spoken in quite a while. Although her hand throbbed, she knew this was the right move.

Self-satisfied, she smirked wondering how long it would take for him to recover and what price she'd have to pay. If she was going to die anyway, might as well get in a shot or two.

"I'm going to enjoy killing you for this," Taric croaked from the floor.

The air shifted somehow. Scuffled sounds infiltrated the normal silence that she'd been living in. It paused leaving Alicia to wonder if she heard it. But the door opened, and shouts rang out, "Police! Hands up."

Alicia imagined, Taric used his hands to self-soothe his balls.

Law enforcement officers swarmed and untied her as a heavyset gentleman strolled in after. Reaching out his hand for a shake, he introduced himself. "I'm Detective Pierzynski."

Tears pooled her eyes, making it hard to see anyone. "Thank you so much. Thank you."

"Next time Faraday tells you to call me before you walk out the house, what are you going to do?"

"Call?"

"That's the only thanks I need."

Alicia leaned in to whisper, "I need you to find a friend of mine."

Pierzynski nodded toward the door. "Our recruit can help with that."

A new officer hurried through the door in what appeared to be full S.W.A.T. gear including a helmet that no one else wore.

She knew that build, that walk. As the other officers helped her sit up, she immediately rushed to the *recruit* as he flipped up his face shield revealing Dallas.

As she rushed into his arms, Dallas hugged her tight before pulling back and checking her over. "Your hand." He gingerly held and turned it, inspecting her injury.

Although it still throbbed, the joy of seeing him eased some of the pain. "Nothing a doctor can't fix."

He pulled her close again and uttered. "You scared me."

"Hell. I scare me." She replied.

Smiling, he held her tighter. "How do you feel about staying one more day?"

"We'll see about my hand. I don't know what to say about this." She waved at the room. "However, I'm counting on your giving me amazing dreams to push out the nightmare I lived through." Her arms tightened around his waist.

"My pleasure." He muttered before leaning down for a kiss.

Thank you for reading 30 Days of Pleasure. If you find my work so captivating that you cannot wait to read another word, purchase your next Sierra Kay novel by visiting bit.ly/authorsierrakay.

Also, use one of the following means to keep in touch.
Newsletter Sign-Up: Sierrakay.com
Facebook: FB.com/authorsierrakay
Instagram: @authorsierrakay
Twitter: sierrakay1

I appreciate your support. Until next time …
~ Sierra Kay

From Behind the Curtain by Sierra Kay

Dee dropped out of high school the moment her mother's battle with cancer took a downward spiral. She became the unlikely breadwinner in a house that had too much pain and not enough money. That also meant dealing with a transient father who struggled with addiction. Dee had more than paid her dues; she had been overcharged by life from the very beginning.

When Auntie M brought Dee to live in Atlanta, things were supposed to be better than life in the Chicago projects. In Atlanta, Dee had new clothes, a full fridge, and her own bedroom. She could finally have a future dictated by opportunity and not circumstance.

However, she soon realized that even this opportunity came with its own price. Something was off about the overdose of Pastor Clifton, her aunt's best friend and secret love. And no one is asking the question how did the community's leader and political activist end up slumped over his desk--dead?

Auntie M finally emerges from her fog of grief ready to get justice, and Dee is more than willing to help. But in a church full of gossips, no one is saying a word. In Dee's world, people who had that kind of power were at least honest about their crimes. But here, in a world of saints it was difficult to distinguish the players and, more importantly, the mastermind who was manipulating everyone from behind the curtain.

In the Midst of Fire by Sierra Kay

When your home is in a place so volatile that the devil himself would give it a wide berth, the only direction you're trying to move … is out.

Seraphina Glen had come up from an average street hustler to a married woman with a prestigious address and two teenage twin stepchildren. She walked away from her old life burning bridges and stomping on the ashes. However, Seraphina's escape was temporary.

Now she finds herself back in her old apartment dragging her husband's failure in a bag with her broken dreams. The twins are struggling with the significant life downgrade. Her husband's depression smothers any lingering happy thoughts that managed to grow like weeds through concrete.

As Seraphina reacquaints herself with the rules of survival, she takes steps that shake the foundation of the ideal family she tried to construct.

When Seraphina's circle becomes a target, what punishment is she willing to dole out and what will she be forced to endure when she finds herself caught up in the midst of fire?

At the Touch of Love by Sierra Kay

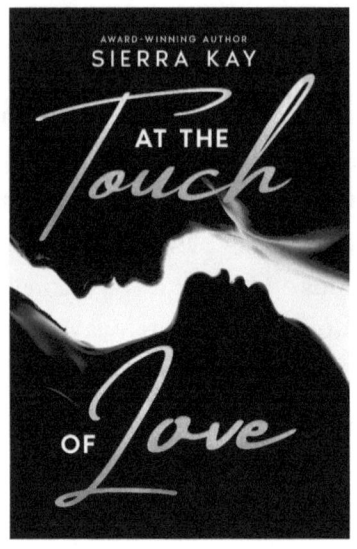

Best friends Echo and Telia are really experiencing some "interesting" times.

Echo received a call on her twenty-first birthday that changed her life forever. Fourteen years later, she gets to add a pink slip to her birthday confetti. She wishes the calendar would skip over this particular day because her mental state won't tolerate one more tragedy. And then the phone rings with news that signals another ungranted birthday wish.

Dr. Daniel Ellington's touch provided the electricity that pumped Telia's heart. However, an accident spared the lives of their children but left his hanging in the balance. Now, Dan's mother has descended on Telia, determined on securing control of his inheritance and heirs using every weapon in her arsenal. Fighting to keep her man, children, as well as her sanity may take everything Telia has, including her life.

As Echo and Telia are thrown into the chaotic fray that is their lives, they soon realize that happy endings are only promised in fairytales.

Sweet Whispers of the Devil by Sierra Kay

Victoria Hill's son is missing—her worst nightmare realized. A nightmare made even more terrifying because, he's in the hands of her father, a bounty hunter intent on connecting with his relations regardless of their attempts to escape his grasp. While Victoria's mother, Honey, had changed their identities and moved from place to place to stay safe, she couldn't prevent Victoria's own kidnapping. Instead, she was forced to sacrifice everything she had to keep Richard at bay.

Now Honey's dead. And daddy's come calling. Again. With the help of an ex-lover and his mother, it's Victoria's turn to make the decisions that could mend her family, save her son, or send Richard over the edge. One problem. The decisions could also force Victoria to change the game in a way that sends them all on a slide straight down into her father's particular brand of hell.

About the Days of Pleasure Series
9 Books * All Standalones * No Cliffhangers

10 Days of Pleasure

Some relationships are made in the storm. Real love survives them. Basketball star Dallas Avery has the world in the palm of his hand and a lifetime of happiness or despair within his grasp. For accomplished businesswoman, Alicia Mitchell, love is a double-edged sword wrought with happiness and pain. Business calls the soulmates to Scotland but a new, more treacherous storm is brewing back home. Can their love weather this latest test, or will a crueler fate prevail?

20 Days of Pleasure

NBA star Dallas Avery has one intention when he visits the most romantic city in the world—win Alicia Mitchell by any means necessary. They relish their time as a couple—free to explore their magnetic connection in Paris and savor the array of pleasures they discover as soul mates.

But family, friends, the media, and society at large, have various opinions about their complicated relationship. Will Dallas and Alicia find a way to stay together, or will the many factors working against them shatter their once-in-a-lifetime romance?

30 Days of Pleasure

Every end is supposed to be a beginning. After the death of her husband, Alicia Mitchell set herself up financially to embrace freedom and see the world. Then she met a detour. Until NBA basketball star Dallas Avery wrapped his arms around her, Alicia didn't know what it felt like to be cherished. Now he's drawing her focus and shifting her priorities. And Alicia doesn't mind. However, there's a shadow creeping from the edges of her dating history.

Taric Hasan, a man she considered dating until she experienced his dark side, has emerged. Although she once managed to escape him, Taric isn't done with her. He's intent on ending their relationship on his terms … with her death.

40 Days of Pleasure

The NBA's sexy and most valuable player Dallas Avery meets the beautiful Alicia Mitchell, who has one thing on her mind: leaving. Their attraction is intense, but the timing is off. Dallas is determined to convince Alicia to give their May-December relationship a chance, but when their romantic trip to the Caribbean gets derailed by them being embroiled in a local family's deadly drama, romance gets put on the back burner.

50 Days of Pleasure

When an obsessive fan threatens to derail Basketball Superstar Dallas Avery's relationship with the alluring and independent Alicia Mitchell, a trip to Canada comes at the opportune time. The historic sites and chilly landscapes help to stir the growing connection between the couple.

Then a distressed infant is thrust into their care. The teenage mother and her baby are in danger and only trust Dallas and Alicia to help. With the local mob in pursuit and Dallas and Alicia unable to depend on the police, they must flee the country using a historic mode of escape.

60 Days of Pleasure

Determined to give Alicia Mitchell the love that she longs for, NBA-star Dallas Avery whisks her away on exciting adventures around the world.

Dallas let his heart dictate their journey to Seattle and allows the Emerald City to work its magic on Alicia. Until civil unrest involving the indigenous people collides with a dirty politician's plans to use city funds to cover personal debts. A chance meeting with Yuma, a tribal chief's son, creates an opportunity for Dallas to make a difference for those whose voices have been silenced. When an altercation with the police develops after Dallas and Alicia assist a homeless woman, Yuma's tribe is forced to shift gears and protect the couple.

Can Dallas keep the love of his life safe, and will the civil unrest drive a permanent wedge between them?

70 Days of Pleasure

Dallas Avery and Alicia Mitchell are off to Nashville, Tennessee for business and pleasure. Unfortunately, the past returns to haunt the basketball superstar and puts both in imminent danger.

Conway Ackerman has spent the last five years in prison, charged with aggravated stalking of the athlete early in his career. A bitter man with a sordid past, and a psychotic personality, Ackerman has recently been let out of prison and has set a course that will exact the perfect revenge.

While Dallas is aware of the convict's release, he keeps Alicia in the dark. The stage is set for a myriad of adventures, which will extend to the iconic Beale Street in Memphis, but danger is in the midst. A race against time ensues as the couple is tracked from place to place. Will they survive or meet their demise at the hands of a man whose mental state is deadly?

80 Days of Pleasure

From a romantic picnic in the Southwest to jet-setting around the globe to exotic destinations, Dallas Avery lays the foundation for a long-lasting relationship with Alicia Mitchell, brick by brick, beginning with these five words, "Just one more day, baby."

While traveling the romantic countryside from Munich, Germany to Schloss Neuschwanstein, a case of mistaken identity threatens their freedom and possibly their lives. Dallas has faced numerous threats, but nothing could have prepared him for this experience. A desire to make Alicia's childhood dream come true has evolved into an incredible nightmare.

Dallas and Alicia struggle to learn the new rules of engagement they have been forced to play by. One thing is certain, the NBA player is determined they will not be on the losing end.

90 Days of Pleasure

Alicia Mitchell, is and was, the only woman Dallas Avery has ever loved. He strives to soothe her fears about their age difference, the unresolved issues of her past, and is determined to make her his forever.

An impromptu trip to Durabia brings more danger to their relationship. Crown Prince Amir sets his sights on Alicia and puts a diabolical plan in motion for her to be secretly brought into the palace where he can have her all to himself. None of them could fathom that a third party would intervene, and plunge Dallas and Alicia in the middle of a brotherly war.

USA TODAY Bestselling Author, Naleighna Kai, tells the dynamic love triangle of a chance encounter that lands wealthy NBA star, Dallas Avery, back in the arms of Alicia, the woman of his dreams. A woman he hasn't seen in years. A woman he soon discovers is his fiancée's long-lost aunt!

But Tori, isn't ready to give up all that she's worked for in their relationship, so she makes him a shocking offer—go through with the wedding and she'll still allow him to be with the one woman he now can't seem to do without. Dallas will get a family, something her aunt can't give him and Tori will have the lifestyle she clamors. And Alicia will embrace the love she's longed for all her life and that had already been in her reach before she disappeared. Everyone will get a little of what they want. . . and maybe a whole lot of what they don't.

The details of the trio's love life play out in the tabloids and on talk shows, making Dallas the center of an NBA scandal. Eventually, the doors slam shut on this open marriage in the making and Dallas is forced to make a choice to end the chaos.

www.ingramcontent.com/pod-product-compliance
Lightning Source LLC
LaVergne TN
LVHW041649060526
838200LV00040B/1765